FOLK TALES FROM ASIA
FOR CHILDREN EVERYWHERE

Book Three

sponsored by the
Asian Cultural Centre for Unesco

New York · WEATHERHILL/HEIBONSHA · *Tokyo*

This is the third volume of Asian folk tales to be published under the Asian Copublication Programme carried out, in cooperation with Unesco, by the Asian Cultural Centre for Unesco / Tokyo Book Development Centre. The stories have been selected and, with the editorial help of the publishers, edited by a five-country central editorial board in consultation with the Unesco member states in Asia.

First edition, 1976

Jointly published by John Weatherhill, Inc., 149 Madison Avenue, New York, New York 10016, with editorial offices at 7-6-13 Roppongi, Minato-ku, Tokyo; and Heibonsha, Tokyo. Copyright © 1976 by the Asian Cultural Centre for Unesco / Tokyo Book Development Centre, 6 Fukuro-machi, Shinjuku-ku, Tokyo. Printed in Japan.

LIBRARY OF CONGRESS CATALOGING IN PUBLICATION DATA: Main entry under title: Folk tales from Asia for children everywhere / Book 3-: lacks series statement / "Sponsored by the Asian Cultural Centre for Unesco" / SUMMARY: A multi-volume collection of traditional folk tales from various Asian countries illustrated by native artists / 1. Tales, Asian / [1. Folklore—Asian] / I. Yunesuko Ajia Bunka Sentā / PZ8.1F717 / 398.2′095 [E] / 74-82605 / ISBN 0-8348-1034-4

Contents

The Carpenter's Son

Once, a long time ago, there was a boy named Salim. His father, who had been a carpenter, was dead. The boy and his mother were very poor and for many years they lived from hand to mouth.

One day, Salim's mother managed to raise a little money by selling her husband's chisel and saw. She gave the money to Salim, saying: "Son, you're grown now. So take this money and go into business with it."

With the money in his pocket, Salim went to the bazaar. There he met a man who had a cat for sale. Using all the money, he bought the cat and took it home.

Salim's mother was astonished. "Here we can hardly feed ourselves," she said. "So how can we feed a cat as well?"

A few days later the mother sold her husband's old shoes. She gave the money to Salim and said: "Buy something better this time."

At the bazaar Salim met a man who had a dog for sale. Again he used all the money and brought the dog home.

His mother was still more upset. "Wasn't a cat enough!" she exclaimed.

A few days later she sold her last possession, an old rug. She gave Salim the money, saying: "Salim, this is our last hope. There's nothing more left to sell. Get something useful this time."

This time at the bazaar Salim met a man with a snake that

had a brightly colored crown on its head. Again he spent all his money and brought the snake home.

His mother was frightened. "What do you mean by spending our last money on a snake?" she cried. "At least the cat catches mice and the dog guards our hut, but what good is a snake? Take it out at once and kill it."

Salim took the snake outside. But when he was about to hit it with a rock, the snake spoke. "Ah, kindhearted one," it said to Salim, "please don't kill me. I'm the son of the King of Snakes. Take me back to my father's palace, and he'll reward you richly."

Salim agreed, and on the way the snake said: "When we get to the palace, my father will ask you what reward you want. Don't ask for anything except the ruby my father carries in his mouth. It's not only the largest and most brilliant of all his jewels, but whoever possesses it will have all his wishes fulfilled."

The King of Snakes was very pleased to have his son safely back. He thanked Salim deeply and promised to give him whatever he wanted.

"There's only one thing I want," said Salim, "and that's the ruby you keep in your mouth."

The king was taken aback. "No, I can't give you the ruby," he said. "Ask for anything else and I'll give it to you."

Again Salim asked for the ruby, and again the king refused. Salim was about to leave the palace without any reward, when the king's son spoke: "Father, Salim saved my life and you promised him anything he wanted. If you won't keep your promise, I'm going to leave too."

The king could not bear to lose his son again; so he gave Salim the ruby.

Salim returned home to his mother with the magic jewel. Then he wished for food and clothes and a better house to live in. No sooner had he made his wishes than he saw their old hut turn into a mansion. He and his mother were wearing beautiful new clothes, and before them there was a table loaded with all kinds of delicious foods and costly wines.

From that day on, Salim and his mother had everything they wanted. One day Salim happened to see the daughter of the king and fell in love with her. As was the custom of the land, Salim sent his mother to ask the king to let his daughter marry her son. But when the king heard that Salim was only a carpenter's son, he refused.

Salim sent his mother to the palace a second time to tell the king that, even if he was only a carpenter's son, he could give the king anything he wanted.

The king laughed and said: "If your son will build me a new palace made of bricks of gold and silver, then I'll give him my daughter for his bride."

The mother brought this message to her son, who made the wish on his ruby. Next morning, when the king awoke, he was amazed to see a beautiful new palace, next to his own, made of gold and silver bricks. So the king kept his promise, and Salim married the princess.

Thereafter Salim lived in the new palace with his beautiful wife, his old mother, the cat, and the dog. One day when he was out hunting he saw an old woman crying bitterly beside a grave. He asked her what was the matter, and she told him she had just lost her only son and had no one to look after her. So the kindhearted Salim felt pity and invited her to come and live in the palace. What he did not know was that the old woman was actually an evil witch who had heard about his ruby and wanted to steal it.

One day, while Salim was away, the old woman asked the princess how Salim had become so wealthy, and the princess told her about the magic ruby.

"May I have just one look at it?" the witch asked. When the princess said she didn't know where her husband kept the ruby, the witch exclaimed: "You don't know! Aren't you his wife?" Then she said, in a whisper: "My dear, you must find out how much your husband loves you. Ask him for the ruby. That will be a true test of his love for you."

When Salim returned, the princess asked him to prove his love by giving her the ruby. He answered: "I love you more than all the treasures of the world." Giving her the ruby, he warned: "But you must guard it very carefully."

The princess showed the ruby to the witch and then locked it away carefully in her jewel box. But no locks were safe against the witch. One night when everyone had gone to sleep, she easily opened the box and stole the ruby. Then she wished on the ruby that the palace would disappear and that Salim's wife and mother should be cast away in distant villages.

When Salim woke up, there was no sign of the palace, nor of his wife and mother. Only his dog and cat remained by him. Feeling very sad, he walked out into the country, followed by the cat and dog. Searching for the jewel, they traveled day and night, hungry and thirsty, passing through many towns and villages. Finally Salim was too tired to go on. But the two faithful animals continued the search for the ruby.

One day the two animals came to a place where a wedding was about to be celebrated. It was the wedding of the son of the King of Rats. Salim's cat caught the rat prince and told him that he would not free him unless the other rats found the magic ruby. Thousands of rats scurried everywhere, and finally a lame rat found the house of the old witch. She was asleep with the jewel gleaming in her mouth. The rat sprinkled some snuff on his tail and flicked it under the witch's nose. She sneezed so hard that the jewel was thrown out of her mouth. Leaping into the air, the rat caught the ruby and fled. Then he brought it to the cat, who finally freed the rat prince.

The cat and dog began their journey back to Salim. Along the way they came to a wide river. The dog gave the cat a ride on his back and began to wade across the river, while the cat held the ruby in his mouth. Halfway across the river, the cat saw a delicious-looking fish swimming by. Forgetting everything, the cat opened his mouth to speak to the dog—and out the jewel popped. It fell right into the fish's mouth, and the fish disappeared into the water.

How the dog scolded the cat for his carelessness! Day after day the two animals sat there by the river, wondering how to recover the ruby. Then one day the cat saw a fisherman pulling up out of the river a fish whose skin was gleaming with a strange red light. This must be the fish who had swallowed the ruby! Swiftly, the cat leaped upon

the fish and ripped it open. There was the ruby gleaming in the fish's stomach.

Again the cat and the dog set out on their journey. This time the dog carried the ruby. He ran as fast as he could, with the cat following. Salim was near death when they finally reached him. He was so delighted to see his faithful dog and cat, and so overjoyed to have the ruby back, that he became well at once. He told the jewel to bring back his palace, with his wife and mother in it. Immediately he found himself in the palace with his loved ones. They kissed one another joyfully and shed tears of happiness.

His wife and mother told him how unhappy they had been because of the witch's treachery. Salim ordered the witch to be brought to him. He said to her: "You've been very cruel to all of us. I'll give you one of two choices: do you want a whip or a horse?"

The old witch answered: "Naturally, I'd prefer the horse."

So Salim had a horse brought. He had his men tie the witch to the horse's tail. Then they whipped the horse, which ran out of the palace and then went galloping across the countryside dragging the old witch behind him.

Thus Salim rid himself of the evil witch forever, and thereafter he and his wife and mother lived happily in the palace, together with the faithful dog and cat.

Retold by Mohammad Reshad Wasa
Translated by Abdul Haq Walah
Illustrated by Nabiwalah Kakar

The Four Puppets

Once upon a time there lived a puppet maker and his wife. They had a son named Aung. One day Aung decided that the time had come for him to leave home and seek his fortune in faraway lands. With his father's permission, he got ready for his travels. His mother fixed him some food that would keep for a long time during his journey, and his father gave him four puppets to keep him company and help him along the way.

The first puppet was carved in the figure of the heavenly being named Deva and was dressed in robes of snowy white and gold that flowed down in folds like fleecy clouds. The second was a figure of an ogre named Yakkha, whose body was sheathed in scales of emerald green, with golden spiky fins sprouting from his shoulders and elbows.

The third puppet was carved to represent a demigod named Zawgyi; his body was aflame with red and gold flecks, and he carried a red wand in his hand. The last puppet was a figure of a hermit named Khema; he wore a simple robe and carried a long staff and an alms bowl.

When he was ready to go, Aung knelt before his parents and bowed down three times with his hands clasped together in the shape of a lotus bud. His parents blessed him, and he began his journey. He carried a strong bamboo pole on his shoulder. On one end of the pole was a bundle of clothing and his food; on the other end hung the four puppets.

On the first day of his journey, as the evening shadows began to fall, Aung found himself in a dark forest. He looked for a place to spend the night. The ground underneath a huge banyan tree looked comfortable. But first Aung went to Deva and asked if he should sleep there.

To his amazement, Deva came to life before his eyes and spoke to him in a kindly voice, saying: "Aung, my boy, you must use your eyes and think for yourself."

Aung looked around carefully and saw the footprints of a tiger under the tree. So he gave up the soft, warm bed of leaves and climbed up into the tree, where he spent a most uncomfortable night. But he was thankful for Deva's advice, for, in the dead of night, a huge tiger and his mate came and sniffed about the tree.

Aung continued his journey, and a few days later he camped on a hill above a mountain road. As he looked about him, he saw a caravan of bullock carts coming down the road. He knew the caravan must be loaded with treasures from faraway lands, and he was suddenly seized by the desire to have all the treasure for himself.

He went to Yakkha and asked how he could get the treasure. Yakkha answered: "Aung, my boy, what you wish for, you can have. Nothing is impossible if you have power and strength. Look!" With that, Yakkha stamped his right foot on the ground, and the earth shook like a ship in a storm. There was a din of crashing boulders and stones and terrified cries as part of the hill crumbled away and blocked the road. The men of the caravan ran for their lives; they went helter-skelter in all directions until they were quite out of sight.

Yakkha said: "There you are, Aung. The men have all fled, and all the treasure is yours for the taking."

Aung ran down to the road. "It's mine, all mine!" he cried. He went from one cart to another, flinging his arms around chests filled with gold and silver, satins and silks, rugs and carpets.

Suddenly he heard the sound of sobbing. Surprised, he looked about him. There, crouching in a cart, he saw a young girl. She was Mala, the daughter of the owner of the caravan, who had been left all alone. Aung tried to comfort her, promising to take care of her. But she became very angry, saying: "Take me if you will, along with all the treasure you're stealing, but I will never speak to you—a robber and a thief!"

Aung didn't know what to do. He was looking for words when Yak-kha said: "Come along now, my boy. There's no time to waste chatting with sobbing girls. Remember, a man must always be firm. Firmness is part of power and strength. Come along now, we have much to do."

It was true. There were many things for Aung to do. Once he had all the wealth he wanted, he must not only keep it but make it grow. So he asked for help from the third puppet, Zawgyi. "Tell me what you can do for me," Aung said to Zawgyi. In answer, Zawgyi leaped into the air and waved his red wand. The magic of the wand unlocked

nature's guarded secrets, and all the elements were tamed and harnessed to serve Aung.

Aung should have been the happiest man in the world, but he was not: Mala would not speak to him. Aung showered her with gifts—all the most beautiful things in the world—but still Mala remained silent and unmoved.

One day Mala did finally speak to him. She told him her old father had come to Aung's palace looking for her. Aung had stolen all his wealth, and he was now very poor. Since the stolen wealth had multiplied many times in Aung's hands, Mala demanded that he should return her father's wealth.

Aung was quite willing to do as she wanted. He had so much money that he could give her old father back all his wealth and even some of the profit it had made. In exchange, he had only one favor to ask: would Mala stay with him?

But Yakkha and Zawgyi strongly opposed his plan. "If you give in once, there'll be no end to it. More demands will surely come," they said. "Remember, in this world of wealth and power, it never pays to be weak; it never pays to give in."

At first Aung tried to argue with them, but Yakkha and Zawgyi

argued all the harder. They shamed him again and again for his weakness. While they were still arguing, a servant came to tell Aung that Mala and her father had left, without even waiting for their treasure.

Only then did Aung realize how unhappy he was, how sad and lonely. Then he remembered the fourth and last puppet that his father had given him so long ago, the hermit Khema. So Aung turned to Khema for advice. The hermit had no strength or power or wealth, just his robes and his staff and his bowl. "But I couldn't care less," he said to Aung. "I do not know unhappiness. I am at peace with the world and therefore at peace with myself."

Aung decided to try the hermit's way of life. He left his palace and wandered throughout the land, living on the alms that kind people gave him. Strangely enough, he was much happier. The only thing he wanted now was to find Mala and her father and humbly ask their forgiveness.

One day he stood at the door of a humble dwelling, waiting for someone to come out and give him alms. He heard steps approaching but kept his eyes lowered. Then, when two hands began putting food into his bowl, he saw the white, blue-veined, tapered fingers that he had so often longed to touch.

Aung raised his head. "Mala!" he cried. "Don't you know who I am? I am Aung, and I have come to ask forgiveness. Where is your father?"

Aung was taken into the house to Mala's father. He humbly begged their pardon, and both Mala and her father readily forgave him. Then they talked of many things, of the past and the present and the future, and finally the father and Mala agreed to go back to Aung's palace with him.

As the three approached the palace gates, they were welcomed by Aung's friends, the four puppets. Deva said: "Welcome home. Now you know what harm wealth and power can do. They will not bring peace and happiness unless you soften the might of Yakkha with wisdom and sweeten the power of Zawgyi with lovingkindness. Now hear what Khema has to say."

"Aung, my boy," the hermit began, "you had wealth and power, but you've seen for yourself that they do not bring happiness. Now that you have them again you will be happy, not because of them, but in spite of them. They bring not good or evil of themselves. It only depends on how you use them. You've learned a great lesson that will guide you the rest of your life."

Aung thanked his friends deeply. He even thanked Yakkha and Zawgyi, because it was not their fault, but his own, that he had been so misled by wealth and power. He was now determined to use his riches for the good and happiness of others.

He built a holy pagoda, and beside it he placed statues of Deva, Yakkha, Zawgyi, and Khema. Pilgrims came from far and near to worship at the pagoda, and Aung and Mala welcomed them all warmly and gave them food and shelter. In this way they lived happily ever after.

Retold by Khin Myo Chit
Illustrated by Ba Kyi

17

The Clever Mouse-deer

One hot afternoon a clever mouse-deer was drinking from a clear lake in the jungle. While he was drinking, a tiger passed by. Seeing the mouse-deer, the tiger stopped. He laughed wickedly and said in his fiercest voice: "Oh ho! Little mouse-deer, what a pleasant meal you will make for me! Hurry and get ready to be my dinner, for I've had nothing to eat all day."

"You've had nothing to eat all day?" said the mouse-deer, pretending to be sorry for the tiger. Actually he was trembling with fear at the sight of the tiger's huge jaws and sharp ivory teeth. But, trying his best not to show it, he continued: "Oh, you poor tiger! Really, I would like you to have a nice dinner, but I don't think a small animal like me could satisfy your appetite."

"But I'm hungry!" roared the tiger, becoming impatient.

"That's it!" cried the mouse-deer, thinking of a plan. "What you need to fill your hunger is the flesh of a man."

"And what is a man, mouse-deer?"

"Don't you know what a man is?" exclaimed the deer, pretending to be surprised.

"No, I don't think I do," said the tiger, beginning to be curious. "Tell me, mouse-deer, what is a man?"

"Well," said the deer, glad that the tiger was falling into his trap, "a man is a kind of animal that has two legs and is the most powerful creature in the world."

"Really? Even more powerful than I?" asked the tiger, rather offended.

"Oh, yes, but if you are very quick, you can pounce on him and eat him for your dinner."

"Fine, but if I don't get a man, then you are what I am going to eat. Is that a bargain?"

"It's a bargain!" cried the deer, pleased.

"But where can I find a man? You must show me at once, for I am famished. If you don't hurry, I shall have to eat you up this very minute!"

"Be patient, great tiger," replied the deer. "Now come with me to the edge of the road, and perhaps we shall see one pass by."

So the mouse-deer led the tiger to the edge of the road, and, hiding behind some bushes, they waited for a man to pass. Soon there came a little boy who was on his way to school. He was so busy thinking of his homework that he didn't notice the two animals spying on him.

"Is that a man?" asked the tiger. "Why, I'm sure I'm much more powerful than he!" he sneered.

"Bah, that's not a man," answered the deer. "That's only a man in the making. He'll need many more years—twenty or more perhaps, and you may be dead by then."

Then an old man walked slowly down the road. He was so old

that his beard was as white as snow, and he used a walking stick to help himself along.

"This must be the man you mean. No wonder he has become so thin after living so many years! You're cheating me again," said the tiger angrily.

"No, no! That's not a man. That's only the leftover of a man. A fine fellow like you wouldn't want to eat leftovers, now would you?"

"No—no, of course not. But neither do I feel like waiting any longer."

"Hush! Here comes a real man!" said the deer, as a stout hunter with a gun came striding along the road. "Look at his plump body that's so full of meat, and his colorful cheeks that have plenty of blood. Surely you wouldn't want to eat me after eating that man, would you?"

"I might, mouse-deer, I might! Now watch me!" And with that the tiger pounced on the hunter. But the hunter was too quick for him. He aimed his rifle and shot the animal on the spot.

So the deer, glad to be safe but very tired from his adventure, went back to the lake to drink. While he was drinking, something suddenly caught him by a leg. He started to yell out, but when he saw who had caught him, he swallowed his pain and began thinking fast.

It was the crocodile, another of his great enemies! The crocodile hated the deer for being so full of tricks, and the deer hated the crocodile for frightening him every time he wanted to drink from the lake. This time he was especially angry, but he hid his feelings and managed

to laugh, saying in a scornful voice: "Oh, you poor crocodile, when are you ever going to learn the difference between a deer's leg and a stick? That's just an ordinary old stick you're holding onto so hard."

But the crocodile was used to the deer's tricks. "Don't try to fool me again," he said. "I know very well it's your leg I'm holding, and I'm not going to let it go until I've eaten you up."

"But I'm not fooling you," said the deer. "If you think I'm playing a trick, then what on earth is this?" And the deer waved another leg before the crocodile's face.

The stupid crocodile then believed what the deer said. Quickly he let go of the leg he had and made a grab for the other leg. But the deer had been waiting for this chance. He leaped away. Then, safely out of reach, he turned and said to the crocodile: "You're really more stupid than a donkey. You can't even tell the difference between my leg and an old stick!"

And with that the deer went running away, leaving the crocodile to sink into the lake again, angry at losing another battle of wits.

Presently he met a snail. He was glad to see the snail because he loved to boast, and now he could boast to the snail. He challenged the snail to a race and was very surprised when the snail accepted. And what was even more surprising was that the snail promised to win. The deer laughed. How could a snail ever dream of winning a race?

But this snail also happened to be cunning. He had earlier planned with a friend how they could outwit the tricky mouse-deer together.

"You'll see how you can win a race with me, slow snail," the deer cried, and he was off like the wind. But when he reached the finish line, he nearly jumped out of his skin to see the snail already there

before him. The deer didn't want to admit that he had lost, so he challenged the snail to start the race again. But no matter how many times he challenged, the snail always won.

Now, what the deer didn't know was that all the time the snail was using his brain. Each time it was a different snail standing at the finish line, first the original snail's friend and then the original snail. The two snails looked so much alike that the deer thought they were one and the same.

Back and forth the deer ran, until he was finally so exhausted that he fell to the ground panting. "You've won, Mr. Snail," gasped the deer. "I give up."

And this is the way the little mouse-deer who thought he was so smart was finally defeated that day—not by the fierce tiger, not by the ferocious crocodile, not by any of the other huge animals of the jungle, but by a tiny, slimy snail!

Retold by Annette K. Hadimaja
Illustrated by Syahwil

22

The Crow and the Fox

Once a crow who lived in a forest decided to raise some babies. So she built a nest high in an elm tree and laid three eggs in it. She set on them for twenty-one days until they finally hatched, and out came three baby crows.

Now that her babies were born, the mother crow became very busy.

She had to feed them all day, for the little ones were always hungry. She also had to protect them, for there were many thieves who were after her nestlings.

One of their enemies was a mean fox who lived not far from the elm tree. When the fox heard the nestlings chirping, he said to himself: "Well, I see there's some food for me in that nest!" He went up to the tree, but the nest was too high for him. Even when he jumped, it was quite beyond his reach. So he thought of ways to catch the nestlings and came up with a plan.

First he looked into the trash cans of a nearby village and found himself an old felt hat. Then he stole an old rusty saw from the forester. Early next morning, before the crow had left her nest, the fox walked up to the elm with the old hat on his head and began to cut down the tree with the rusty saw.

Startled by the sound of the saw, the crow looked down from the nest and asked: "Who are you, and what are you doing?"

"Oh, I'm the forester, and I'm going to cut down my tree," the cunning fox replied.

"Please don't cut this tree down. My nest is here and my little ones are in it," said the crow.

"You've done wrong to build your nest in my tree," said the fox, "for I want to cut the tree down right now."

The crow began to moan. "Please give me a few days' time so that my little ones can grow and gain strength," she begged.

"No, not even an hour," the fox said. "This is my tree and I want to cut it down right now."

The crow went on pleading. "Please give me two days, then," she said, "for my little ones to learn how to fly. Then we'll all leave the tree."

"I can't be bothered by what you say. All I know is that the tree belongs to me and I want to cut it now." With these words the fox began sawing again. The crow started crying. She didn't know what to do.

Then the fox, casting a sly glance at the nest from under the felt hat, said: "Well, all right. I'll give you two days. But then you must give me one of your nestlings. I'll wait only on that condition."

The poor crow had to agree. The fox devoured the baby crow at once. He was pleased that his trick had worked, and even more

24

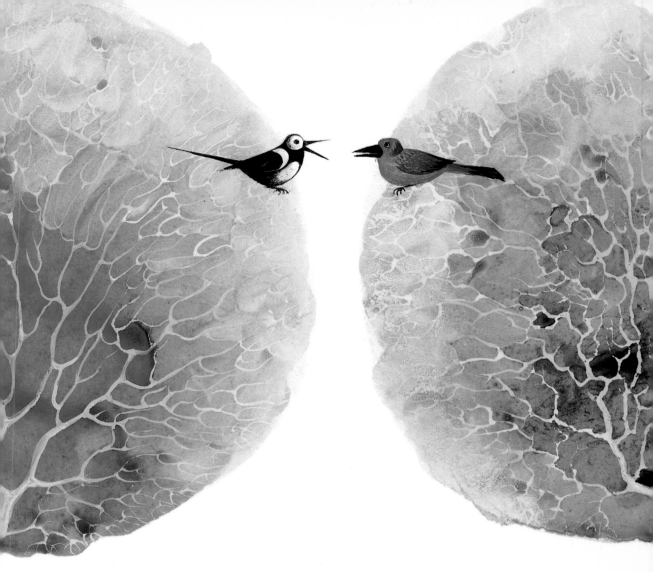

pleased to think that from now on he could play the same trick on other birds as well.

After the fox had left, a magpie who was the crow's neighbor came to visit her. Seeing the crow deep in sorrow, the magpie asked: "What's the matter with you?"

The crow told her the whole story.

"That's funny," said the magpie. "A forester never cuts down a green, shady tree. You must have been tricked. Well, next time he comes, show him to me, and I'll tell you if he is a true forester or not."

Two days later, feeling very proud, the fox came back again with the old hat on his head and the rusty saw under his arm.

As soon as she saw the hat, the crow flew to the magpie to tell her that the forester was there. The magpie carefully examined him and said: "You ignorant creature! That's no forester, that's the tricky fox. You were fooled by his hat and his saw. Well, don't be afraid. If he tells you that he wants to cut down your tree, tell him to go ahead. He couldn't possibly cut down the tree. He would need a sharp double-edged saw and strong arms to do so."

26

Just as the fox started sawing, the crow returned to the tree. "Who are you, and what are you doing?" she asked.

"I'm the forester, and I'm going to cut down my tree," the fox answered.

"Go ahead and cut it down if you think you can," said the crow. "I'm not leaving my nest. And you're not a forester either. You're the mean fox!"

The fox was surprised by the great change that had come over the crow. The day before yesterday she was all moaning and begging, but today she was all defying. He knew at once that somebody had warned the crow of his trick.

"Who told you I'm not a forester?" asked the fox, determined to find out who it was.

Now the crow made a mistake and told him that it was the magpie. The fox then promised himself to take revenge on the magpie.

After a few days passed, the fox went into a gutter and made himself dirty. Then he came and lay down under the tree where the magpie had her nest. He stayed there quietly, pretending to be dead.

The magpie saw him. She passed by him twice, but the fox remained motionless. "He must be dead," thought the magpie to herself. "Now I'd better peck out his eyes."

She flew down to the fox's body and pecked at his ribs. The fox did not move. So she came and sat on his head. But as she was about to peck his eyes, the fox suddenly caught her between his jaws.

The magpie knew she was trapped. But she too was clever. She said to the fox: "You have every right to kill me, for it was I who taught the crow and other birds about your tricks. I am as clever as you and know many tricks myself. Now think. You can eat me now. But that'll fill your stomach just for a day. Or you can let me go and make me your friend; then I can teach you my tricks. They will make your life easier for the rest of your days."

The fox thought about it. Maybe she is right. The magpie is a clever bird, and friendship with her would surely be to my advantage. Perhaps she can help me to get a couple of birds a day.

"Make up your mind," the magpie said. "If you want us to be friends, you must promise now by the sunshine, by the light of the moon, and by the god of the forest that we'll be friends."

The fox opened his mouth to make the promise. The next moment

27

the magpie had escaped and flown to the top of the tree, leaving the fox shaking his head sadly. Cunning as he was, he had to admit that this time it was he who had been tricked.

But the magpie was not done. Next day she called all the birds of the forest to gather together and get rid of the fox once and for all. While the fox was sleeping by a pond, the great swarm of birds suddenly descended upon him, pecking him with their beaks and scratching him with their claws. The fox was so frightened that, when he tried to run away, he took the wrong direction and fell into the pond and was drowned.

Translated by Golnar Ganjei
Illustrated by Nooredin Zarrinkelk

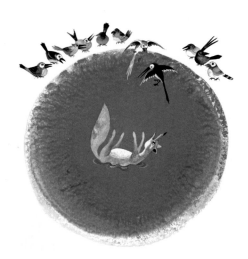

The Story of Urashima Taro

Once upon a time, in a small village by the sea, there lived a young fisherman named Urashima Taro. Every day, no matter what the weather, Taro went out fishing, for he supported his aged parents by selling the fish he caught.

One day Taro set out to sea in his small boat as usual. It was a stormy day. The strong north wind was blowing and the sea was rough. Though he worked hard, he caught almost nothing. Nonetheless, Taro stayed in his boat till evening. But all he had in his basket at the end of the day were three small fish.

Discouraged, Taro drew his boat up onto the beach and started home. On his way he saw several village children gathered around something on the beach. Shouting noisily, the children were poking at the thing with sticks. Wondering what they were playing with, Taro went over to see. It was a beautiful little turtle whose shell shone in

five different colors. The children were tormenting it. Some were pounding on its shell, and the others were trying to turn it over.

"Don't do that," said Taro. "Let it go."

But the children paid no attention. They began to beat the poor creature all the harder. But when Taro offered his three fish in exchange for the turtle, the children agreed to let it go.

Taro put the turtle down carefully at the edge of the water. "Now go home safely. Don't come back here, for the bad children might catch you again," said Taro.

The turtle swam into the water and, looking back at Taro again and again as if to thank him, disappeared beneath the waves.

Taro went home with an empty basket.

The next day, the sea was stormy again. But Taro went out fishing, determined to fill his basket. At noon the basket was empty. And at evening it was still empty. He hadn't been able to catch even one fish all day.

Before he finally gave up, he cast his line out once again, thinking that this would be his last try for the day. Suddenly there was a heavy pull on his line, which bent his rod almost double. With all his strength Taro pulled on the line. As he pulled, he saw something shining at the end of the line. It became brighter and brighter until at last a beautiful maiden appeared from beneath the waves, followed by a huge turtle.

The maiden gently spoke to Taro, who was speechless with surprise. "I am the little turtle that you rescued yesterday. In reality, I am the daughter of the King of the Sea. Today I came to thank you for your kindness and invite you to my father's palace under the sea. My father the king wishes to see you. Please come with me." So saying, the princess took Taro by the hand and seated him on the back of the turtle, who dived quietly beneath the waves.

With each stroke of the turtle's legs, Taro went deeper and deeper into the sea. The water around him became darker and darker until they came to a thick tangle of seaweed.

"Please shut your eyes and hold on tightly," said the princess to Taro.

Taro took a firm grip on the turtle's back and closed his eyes as he was told. It seemed that they passed through a long jungle of seaweed. Taro felt the trailing weeds clutching at him one after another.

30

Finally the princess said: "Now you may open your eyes."

When Taro opened his eyes, it was no longer dark, and there before him stood a magnificent palace glowing with a strange light. As the princess and Taro came up to the gate, the doors swung open and a multitude of fish in different shapes and colors swam out. The princess led Taro through the gate.

The King of the Sea greeted Taro warmly and thanked him for rescuing his daughter. Soon a marvelous feast was laid to welcome Taro. Beautiful fish danced gracefully to entertain him.

The King of the Sea said to Taro: "Now that you have come to the world beneath the sea, you no longer belong to the world of men. You belong to our world. Marry my daughter and stay here, and you will be happy forever."

Taro was captivated by the wonder of the world beneath the sea. Forgetting all about his parents, his fishing, and the life above, he consented to stay. The banquet now turned into the wedding feast.

More dishes were brought in. The music and dancing became merrier, and the feast continued for a long time.

Thus three happy years passed for Taro in the kingdom under the sea. It was all like a beautiful dream. Then one day, the princess took Taro into a room he had never seen before.

The room had four windows, one on each side. When Taro opened the window on the east side, it was spring outside. The cherry trees were in full blossom and the birds were singing merrily. When he opened the one on the south, it was summer. Flowers of all kinds were blooming and the cicadas were chirping. Outside the western window, it was autumn. The leaves were changing color and the voices of deer could be heard. The northern window showed Taro his native village in winter. There was his old house and the ocean where he used to fish. It was snowing hard and the north wind was blowing.

All of a sudden Taro remembered his aged parents and his life above the sea. He was seized with homesickness. Taro wished to go back. "I've been very happy here," he said to the princess, "but I want to return home now."

At first the princess tried to dissuade him. But when she saw that Taro's mind was firmly made up, she presented him with a beautiful box and said: "Please take this box with you. This is a magic box. As long as you keep it, we might be able to see each other again. But remember that you must never, never open the box."

Taro accepted the box. The huge turtle who had brought him to the palace was at the gate ready to take him back. Carrying the box under his arm, Taro seated himself on the back of the turtle, who soon brought him back to the beach of his old village.

The seashore was the same as always. But the houses appeared different. So did the people. Taro felt uneasy. He hurried to the place where his house had stood. To his great astonishment he discovered that the house was no longer there.

He walked along until he met an old man whom he did not recognize. "Do you know what happened to the house of Urashima Taro that used to stand over there?" he asked.

"Urashima Taro?" echoed the old man. "Oh, yes," he said after a long while, "yes, I've heard about him. Three hundred years ago there was a young man by that name who lived in this village. But one day he went out to sea and never returned. People say he must

have gone to the kingdom beneath the sea."

Three hundred years ago! Taro was shocked to hear these words. Confused, he wandered off toward the beach. There, sitting on the sand all alone, he fell into deep thought. How could he have been gone so long? He had been in the kingdom beneath the sea for only three years. He couldn't understand. Nor did he know what to do. His eyes fell on the box that the princess had given him. Forgetting what she had said, Taro opened the box.

Three thin columns of smoke floated up out of the box. And the next moment Taro was no longer a young fisherman. He had turned into an old, old man with wrinkled skin and a long white beard.

Retold by Shiro Tokita
Translated by Kyoko Matsuoka
Illustrated by Daihachi Ota

Who is the Provider?

A proud king had seven daughters of dazzling beauty and pure in-
nocence. He loved them dearly, especially the seventh and youngest.
She was not only the most beautiful of all but was also the best cook
in the entire kingdom. Every morning, before holding court, the king
would call his daughters and ask: "Say, my beloved daughters, who
provides all that you have to eat?" Six of them would immediately
answer: "King, our father, it is you who provides our food." But the
seventh princess always remained silent.

One day the king insisted that the seventh princess reply as well.
She said: "Father, God is the provider of all. Everything we have,
everything we eat, we get from him."

This reply enraged the haughty king.
"Get out!" he cried, and he had a servant take the princess away and leave
her deep in the jungle.

As the girl sat in the jungle, brooding

on her misfortune, she fell asleep. In the morning she was awakened by the soft, sweet melody of a flute. She opened her eyes and saw a young man playing a flute.

When she asked how he happened to be in the jungle, he replied: "I herd my master's buffaloes, and yesterday I lost one of them. So I'm afraid to go home and I keep playing my flute to attract the lost buffalo. But, beautiful princess, how do you happen to be here in the jungle?"

She replied: "I can't go home either. Why don't you become my attendant, and we'll go together to find some place to live."

The young man agreed and they set out to the east. Hungry and thirsty, they traveled all day. Just as the shadows became long and the wind cool they came to the walls of a city.

The princess said: "Go into the city and find the richest jeweler there. Tell him a princess awaits him outside the walls."

Soon the boy came back, accompanied by the city's richest jeweler. In exchange for her lovely necklace of rare and precious stones the jeweler gave the princess all she asked for—a saddled horse for herself, some money, and for the young man a robe befitting a royal attendant.

The princess and the young man continued traveling. Finally they reached a place they liked, and the princess decided to have a small palace of her own built there. She also taught the simple buffalo herder the arts of combat and the arts of peace.

One day, while they were on an outing, the princess said to the young man: "Please find me some water to drink or I'll die of thirst."

The young man promptly went in search of water. God is the provider, and soon the young man found a stream of cold water. He filled a cup and was about to leave when he saw beautiful sparkling rubies lying on the bottom of the stream. He picked up some and tucked them into the folds of his turban.

After another moon and a half the palace was finished, and the princess and her attendant moved into it. He often took the rubies out of his turban and played with them. One day the thought occurred to him that if he followed the stream he could find the source of such beautiful jewels.

The stream led him farther and farther to the east, until he found himself standing before the walls of a great palace. The stream flowed under the walls. He crept inside and wandered about. The palace seemed to be empty. Finally he opened a gate into an inner courtyard through which the same stream ran. There beside the stream lay the head of a beautiful woman, with blood dripping from it. The drops of blood were becoming sparkling rubies as they fell into the water. Nearby lay the woman's headless body.

He started to run away but tripped over a plank that was lying on the ground. Instantly the severed head flew through the air and re-joined the body, bringing the woman back to life.

The woman looked at the horrified young man with pity and said: "Lad, what fate has brought you here? Run for your life, or else the genie will find you and tear you apart."

The young man took courage and asked: "Who are you?"

"I am the daughter of the King of Fairies," replied the woman. "My name is Lal Pari, or Red Fairy. The genie who owns this palace wants to marry me, but I hate him. So he has imprisoned me here. Every morning, before he goes out to hunt, he puts me on this magic plank and my head comes off. Then when he returns in the evening, he brings me back to life. I hear him coming now. Quick, put the plank back into place so that I'll die again, and then hide yourself from his anger."

The young man did as Red Fairy ordered, and he had just hidden himself when the genie rushed in, roaring: "I smell man! I smell man!"

38

Quickly he brought the woman back to life and said: "I smell man and I'm very hungry. Tell me where the man is so I can eat him." But Red Fairy pretended not to know. So the genie put her to death again and went out to continue his hunt.

As soon as the genie was out of sight, the young man crept out of his hiding place and brought the woman back to life with the magic plank. They discussed plans for their escape. Red Fairy asked him to go down into a small dark room, where he would find a parrot in a golden cage. "When the genie goes out hunting, he leaves his soul in this parrot, and without his soul he would die," she explained. "Quick, bring me the parrot."

No sooner had the young man brought the parrot than the world suddenly seemed to shake with thunder and storm. In a burst of smoke the genie appeared, maddened with rage. Surely he was going to kill them both. But Red Fairy quickly took the parrot from its cage and strangled it. Instantly the evil genie fell to the ground, dead as a stone.

Thus they were able to escape from the genie's palace, carrying the magic plank with them. The young man took Red Fairy home with him. The princess welcomed her warmly, and soon the two women came to be like sisters. Every night Red Fairy would lie on the magic plank, her head would come off her body, and the blood would form heaps of gleaming rubies of matchless beauty. Every morning they would move the plank, and Red Fairy would come to life again.

After a while Red Fairy decided to go on a long journey. Before leaving, however, she built a new palace for the princess with the help of the magic plank, and they invited many guests to a great feast in the new palace. Among the guests was the king who was the princess's father. The princess herself cooked all his favorite dishes for the feast.

When all the guests sat down to the feast, the king began to weep, tears rolling down his beard. The taste of the delicious food had reminded him of his daughter who in days gone by had prepared just such food for him. How often had he regretted sending her away, and how often had he searched the jungle for her without success.

Red Fairy asked the king the cause of his grief. He told her what had happened, and she asked: "But, sir, do you still love your daughter?"

The king said: "Yes, my only wish is to see her once more before I die."

For an answer, Red Fairy snapped her fingers, and, lo and behold! there before his eyes stood the princess, his lost daughter, now a full-grown woman, neither seventh nor youngest in wisdom.

The two embraced each other and wept. At last the princess fell to her knees and said: "O King, my father, is it not God the Benign, God the Merciful, who is the provider of all things? Look how he has given me this palace and a great treasure of rubies, whereas you could not even find one lost daughter."

The king realized how mistaken he had been. "Yes," he said, "God is indeed the provider of all." And the king and his daughter lived happily ever after.

Retold by Ahmed Basheer
Translated by Iqbal Jatoi
Illustrated by B. A. Najmee

Badang the Strong

Once in the kingdom of Johore there was a slave named Badang. He worked hard in the forest every day, clearing land for his master by cutting down trees and then digging up the roots. In his spare time he set a trap in a nearby river to catch fish.

One day he was disappointed to find his trap empty. But when he looked closer, he saw some scales and bones at the bottom. So there had been some fish in the trap and someone must have eaten them!

Day after day he set his trap, but the same thing happened: the trap was always empty except for some scales and fish bones left in it. "I'm going to find out who's stealing my fish," Badang said. So one day, after he had set his trap, he hid among some tall reeds by the river bank and waited. The water grew cold but he did not move. For a long time he waited, watching the trapped fish swimming about trying to escape. At last he saw someone sneaking up to his trap.

It was a demon with blood-red eyes, hair that was thick and matted, and a beard that hung down almost to his waist. As the demon began eating the fish, Badang sprang at him.

"So you're the thief who's been stealing my fish!" cried Badang, seizing the creature by the beard.

The demon tried to escape, but Badang held him fast. "Don't kill me! Don't kill me!" pleaded the demon. "If you spare my life, I'll grant you anything you wish—riches, power, strength, invisibility—anything. Only, please don't hurt me."

Badang thought quickly. If he was granted riches, his master would take all of them from him. What he needed was strength. If he was strong and powerful enough to uproot trees with a single tug, he could clear the land within a short time. "I want strength," he said, "strength enough to pull up the biggest of trees with one hand."

"Your wish is granted," said the demon. "Now please let me go."

But Badang would not set him free till he had tested his strength. Pulling the demon along with one hand, he went into the forest and took hold of the biggest tree there. The tree was so huge that it would

42

usually have taken him days to cut it down and dig out its roots. But now it came out of the ground, roots and all, as easily as though it were a weed. He was indeed strong! So he let the demon go.

Badang continued to work in the forest. But now, because of his great strength, he could do in a few minutes what it took others days and months to do. The great trees went flying, and in no time the thick forest was a plain, ready for plowing. When his master asked how he had accomplished such wonders, Badang told him the whole story.

"When the demon said he'd grant any wish that I had," Badang concluded, "I chose strength so I could serve you better."

The master was so moved by Badang's words that he granted him his freedom then and there.

Badang's fame spread throughout the land, and not long afterward

the rajah of the nearby island of Singapura invited him to become one of his war chiefs. Badang accepted the offer and performed many great feats of strength for the rajah. Now, when the rajah of the kingdom of Kalinga heard about Badang the Strong he sent his strongest man to challenge Badang. The contest took place in the grounds of the royal palace of Singapura. A great crowd of people gathered and the rajah himself came to watch. It was agreed that the rajah of the champion who was defeated would give the winner seven ships filled with treasure.

In front of the palace there was a huge rock. The Kalinga champion challenged Badang to see who could lift it.

"Very well," said Badang. "You try first."

The Kalinga champion placed his two arms around the rock and lifted with all his might. Inch by inch he raised the rock till it was as high as his knees. But he could not hold it any longer, and the rock fell to the ground with a heavy thud.

"Now it's your turn," the Kalinga champion said to Badang.

Badang stood upright by the rock. Then he bent and lifted the rock high over his head, as easily as though it were a small stone. Swinging around several times, he hurled the rock and sent it sailing far over the heads of the crowd.

How the people cheered!

So Badang won the seven ships filled with treasure, and the defeated champion, crestfallen, sailed for home.

Stories of Badang's great feats of strength reached the kingdom of Perlak. The rajah of Perlak was the younger brother of the rajah of Singapura, and he decided to send his champion, Benderang, to challenge his brother's strong man. He also sent his chief minister to deliver a letter to his brother.

When they arrived on the island, the chief minister, Benderang, and their party formed a colorful procession as they went to the palace to deliver the letter. The leaders rode in state on elephants while their attendants walked beside them.

The chief minister bowed low and handed the letter to the rajah of Singapura. He said: "Your Highness's brother sends his greetings and asks that your champion and his champion have a contest of strength. If your Badang wins, my master will give Your Highness a storehouse full of treasure."

"And if Benderang wins?" asked the rajah.

"Then Your Highness will give the same to my master," said the chief minister.

The rajah of Singapura looked at Benderang, who was much bigger than Badang and seemed remarkably strong. "I will think about it," said the rajah, "and let you have my decision tomorrow."

Later the rajah sent for Badang and asked him if he thought he could win such a match. "It is hard to say," said Badang. And then he made a suggestion: "Perhaps a feast could be held tonight at which I could secretly test Benderang's strength. If he seems too strong for me, then Your Highness could refuse permission to hold the contest and no one will lose honor."

The rajah thought the suggestion sensible. That night a great banquet was laid for the guests. Everyone sat cross-legged on the floor, and while they were making merry, Badang went to sit next to Benderang. Benderang laid his thigh over Badang's and pressed it down with all his might. Badang easily raised his thigh and forced Benderang's up. Then quickly he laid his thigh over Benderang's. Try as he might, Benderang could not raise his thigh. No one was aware of this secret contest between the two champions.

When the guests had gone back to their ship, the rajah asked

Badang what he thought. "Let me fight Benderang," he replied. "I'm sure I can beat him."

At the same time, back on the ship, Benderang was talking to the chief minister. "Sir," he said, "that Badang is extremely strong. If it is possible, please call off the contest. I'm afraid he might beat me."

Early the next morning the rajah entered the audience hall, where the chief minister of Perlak was waiting. The rajah was about to announce the contest when the chief minister said: "Your Highness, after all, it would not be wise to match Benderang against Badang. Whichever one wins, it would seem as if Your Highness and Your Highness's brother were competing against each other, and one of you would lose honor."

The rajah smiled. He knew that the chief minister was in fact admitting that Badang was the stronger man. "Very well," he said, "if such is your wish, so let it be."

The visitors left Singapura and returned to Perlak. The rajah of Perlak did not say anything about the contest that did not take place, for the chief minister had brought him a very friendly letter from his elder brother, the rajah of Singapura.

After that, no one challenged Badang. People everywhere, near and far, admitted that the strongest man in the world was none other than Badang, the ex-slave, from the little island of Singapura.

Retold by Violet Wilkins
Illustrated by George Paul

Mahadena-mutta

Long, long ago there was a little village. The villagers were very simple or often even foolish folk, and they took all their problems to an old man whom they called Mahadena-mutta, which means Great Counselor.

Now, Mahadena-mutta was

tall, strong, and well built. His long hair was tied in a knot at the back of his head and he adorned it with a curved tortoise-shell comb that looked very much like a crown. His beard was white and long, giving him a wise, saintly look. Whenever he went out he always dressed up grandly in a black coat and a colorful shawl. In short, he made a very impressive appearance, and the villagers thought him a very wise man.

He had five faithful followers, whom he called his disciples. Each of them looked quite different, and each had a name to suit his features. Half Coconut had a flat, round face. Pot Belly was short and had a big stomach, while Needle Waist always looked as though he were starving. Palm Tree was tall and skinny. And Big Mouth, whose mouth was always hanging open, looked flabby and dumb. Wherever the master went, these five always followed after, carrying such things as the master's umbrella, his bag of betel, and a book made of palm leaves in which to preserve his words of wisdom.

The master was unhappy at having only five followers. So one day he said to them: "Come, we'll go and look for more disciples. If pupils don't come to the teacher, the teacher must go to the pupils."

Early next morning Mahadena-mutta, with his five followers trailing after him, set out from the village to look for more disciples. They walked for miles and miles. Suddenly realizing that his head had become lighter, the master felt his hair and found his comb was missing.

"Where is my comb?" he shouted in surprise.

"O Wise One, we saw it fall along the way," the five answered in chorus.

"You fools! Why didn't you pick it up?" he asked angrily.

"O Great One," Half Coconut answered humbly, "you have never told us what we should do in such a situation. If you had, we would have written it down in our book and done as you wished."

"All right, all right," said the master impatiently. "Hereafter pick up anything that falls."

So Half Coconut took the palm-leaf book and wrote down his master's words. Then the five of them ran back for miles and found the master's comb where it had fallen. He was very pleased to have it returned to him.

They continued walking, and some time later Mahadena-mutta noticed that each of his disciples was carrying a heavy bag that he

49

hadn't had before. "What's in those bags?" he asked. "Following your words of wisdom, master, we have collected everything that fell on the wayside," they answered proudly. "Oh, you fools!" said the master angrily, "you've not understood me at all. You're supposed to pick up only things that *I* drop." These words too were added to the book, and they continued their journey happily.

When it began to grow dark, they decided to spend the night in a hut they found along the road. Needle Waist climbed a tree to cut some branches for firewood. Sitting astride a branch, he started cutting it at a point between himself and the trunk of the tree.

A passer-by, seeing what Needle Waist was doing, called up to him: "Be careful or you'll come down with the branch, my friend."

"You mind your own business," Mahadena-mutta called out angrily, "and we'll mind ours."

Sure enough, just as the stranger had said, in a moment down came both the branch and Needle Waist, crashing to the ground. Fortunately Needle Waist was not badly hurt. The stranger went on his way while Needle Waist was still brushing himself off.

"That stranger is certainly a clever soothsayer," said Half Coconut. "Just see how quickly what he said has come true."

"Yes, indeed," said the master. "Go ask him when I shall die."

In a flash the five disciples were running after the stranger. But this frightened the man, and he began running even faster than the disciples.

"Stop! Stop! Clever soothsayer," they shouted. "Please tell us when our master will die."

Looking back over his shoulder, the man shouted back: "When his head becomes cold, you fools." And he ran on.

The disciples came back to their master and told him what the man had said. Mahadena-mutta thought for a moment and then, nodding his head wisely, said: "My head will become cold only if I get it wet. Ha, ha! I'll cheat Death by never wetting my head."

But he lay awake all night worrying about the stranger's words. Next morning, giving up his search for new disciples, he led his little band home. From that day on he was very careful not to let his head get wet. But he still went about helping the poor villagers whenever they asked his advice.

One day it happened that a goat wandered into the courtyard of a

farmer's house and put its head into a large clay pot looking for water to drink. Unfortunately, the goat's head became stuck in the pot. With the pot on its head, the frightened goat ran back and forth, bleating loudly. The farmer and his neighbors came running up to see what the commotion was. "Somehow we must save both the goat and the pot," they said. But they didn't know how to do it.

"Let's get Mahadena-mutta's advice," they said and went running off to their Great Counselor.

Mahadena-mutta listened patiently to their story. Then, nodding his head, he said: "It is indeed a problem. I must go and see for myself."

So he set out, riding on an elephant. When he reached the farmer's house, he discovered that the gate into the courtyard was too narrow for the elephant.

"Pull the wall down," he ordered. And once this was done he rode on into the courtyard and looked down at the goat with the pot on its head.

"Well, well!" he said. "Cut off the animal's head and we'll save the pot."

"Cut off the goat's head!" the villagers shouted. And the farmer, with one blow of a sharp knife, did so.

The farmer looked in the pot and said, puzzled: "But the goat's head is still inside the pot."

"Well, smash the pot and take it out," said Mahadena-mutta.

Someone smashed the pot, and everyone cheered the Great Counselor's wisdom. Then they watched in awe and wonder as Mahadena-mutta began trying to figure how to get out of the courtyard, which was too small for the elephant to turn around in.

Mahadena-mutta thought deeply and then said: "Tear down the other wall. Then the elephant can take me home."

Quickly they tore down a second wall, and as the elephant strode through the gap the villagers all whispered among themselves: "He is truly a great man. He is indeed the wisest of the wise."

Pleased with himself, Mahadena-mutta said: "You're such fools that you couldn't get along without me."

In a happy mood, he rode on toward home, with his five followers trailing after, until he came to a river. "A dip in the river will refresh me," he thought. It was such a hot day that he forgot all about keep-

ing his head dry. He climbed off the elephant, dived into the water—
and came up with his head soaking wet.

"Oh! Your head is wet, Wise One," cried his disciples.

Mahadena-mutta felt his head and was overcome with fear at find-
ing it wet. Thinking that his end was near, he climbed onto the bank,
stretched himself out, and lay there silently, as though already dead.

His faithful followers sat around him wailing and weeping for a long
time. Later in the day they made a stretcher of some thick sticks and
placed their master's body on it. Then, covering the body with a white
cloth, they began carrying it to the graveyard. Presently they came to
a crossroads. Not being sure which road led to the graveyard, they
stopped and began arguing.

Hearing their quarrel, Mahadena-mutta became angry and impatient. Quietly he raised his head, stretched out a pointing hand, and
said in a soft voice: "When I was alive, I used to take that road to the
graveyard."

Thinking it was a dead man speaking, the disciples were horrified. They dropped the stretcher to the ground and ran away as fast as their legs would carry them.

"Fools!" said Mahadena-mutta, as he picked himself up and began walking slowly home. He lived for many, many years longer, still followed faithfully by Half Coconut, Pot Belly, Needle Waist, Palm Tree, and Big Mouth. And he still gave wise advice to the villagers whenever a problem arose. But he never let his head get wet again.

Retold by Chandraratne Mahatantila
Translated by R. M. Abeysekara
and A. B. Weerasekara
Illustrated by Sumana Dissanayaka

Big Liar

Once upon a time, there was a boy called Big Liar. He was a clever boy, but as his name tells you, he used most of his cleverness for telling lies. He enjoyed fooling other people around him. No one escaped from being the victim of his lies, not even his aunt and uncle who brought him up after the death of his parents.

One day his uncle went out to plow a field that was some distance away from their house, while his aunt stayed home to do her housework. As he watched his aunt working busily in the kitchen, Big Liar suddenly thought of another trick he could play on his aunt and uncle. He stole out of the house and ran to the field where his uncle was working.

"Uncle, Uncle!" he called when he got to the field. "Come home this minute! Aunt fell down from the ladder. She's bleeding badly. I don't know what to do."

Without a word, his uncle began to run toward home. Then Big Liar took a shortcut and got home before his uncle.

He dashed into the house and shouted: "Aunt, Aunt! Uncle was attacked by a buffalo in the field. It looks as if the animal stuck its horns through his belly. Go quickly or he'll die!"

Before he had finished these words, his aunt was already out of the house. Watching her back, Big Liar grinned happily and went behind the house to hide.

The aunt ran. She ran as fast as her two legs could carry her, but still she felt she was not running fast enough. Then, just when she turned a corner of the road, she almost ran into someone. It was her own husband breathing hard and sweating. The two looked at each other dumbfounded.

"That Big Liar!" They immediately understood that they had been tricked by their nephew again.

The aunt and uncle were furious. "This will be the last time we let that rascal fool us," said the uncle.

They went home and found Big Liar hiding behind the house. Then

55

they put him into a large bamboo cage and fastened the lid tightly. "Stay there till sunset," said his uncle. "Then your aunt and I will carry the cage to the river and throw it into the water so that you can never tell another lie."

At the end of the day, his uncle and aunt carried the cage to the river. But the moment they started to throw it into the water, Big Liar cried out: "Dear Uncle and Aunt, I know I was wrong. So I'm ready to be punished. But please do me a last favor. I have a book called *The Art of Telling Lies,* which I have secretly kept behind the rice basket in the house. May I have it with me now so I can read it in Hell?"

Neither his uncle nor aunt had the heart to refuse this last wish of their nephew's. Besides, the uncle was curious to know what the book said. So they went home to fetch it.

While Big Liar waited in the cage, a blind man came walking along the river bank. The boy called out: "Dear Mr. Blind Man, please come over here if you want to see again." The blind man heard the voice and made his way to the cage. "Quick, now," said the boy, "unfasten the lid of this basket and I'll tell you how to cure your blindness." The blind man fumbled about the cage and finally managed to open the lid. No sooner was it open than Big Liar jumped out and ran away.

When his uncle and aunt came back to tell him that they couldn't find the book, the boy was no longer in the cage. Instead, there stood

56

a poor blind man who was waiting to learn how to cure his eyes. They had been deceived once again!

Big Liar ran into a heavy thicket of bamboo near the river. While he was wandering around in the thicket, he happened to find an old pot full of gold. What good luck! He brought the gold home to his aunt and uncle.

Thanks to the treasure, the family became very rich. The aunt and uncle now realized that no amount of scolding would make the boy mend his ways. Perhaps, they thought, if we marry him to a good girl, the boy might stop telling lies and idling about. So they married their nephew to a young girl in the village. It seemed for a while that marriage had solved the problem, but a few months later his uncle and aunt died, and Big Liar began to go about telling lies and cheating people just as he had before.

One day he was wandering in a forest and found some tiger cubs lying in the grass. Being a very bad young man, he caught the cubs and broke their paws. When the cubs cried out with pain, there came a terrifying roar from somewhere nearby. It must be the mother of the cubs! Big Liar quickly hid himself behind a bush. The next moment

the tigress was there. When she found why her babies were suffering, she carried each of them to the foot of a small tree with green leaves. She bit off some of the leaves from the tree, chewed them, and put the chewed leaves on the broken paws of her babies. To Big Liar's surprise, the cubs were healed within a few minutes.

The boy waited until the tigers were gone. Then he dug up the tree and brought it home. He planted it in his yard and gave it the name of banyan. From that day on, he took great care of the tree. He told his wife that the tree had been given to him by a god and that its leaves could heal all wounds, cure all sickness, and even bring

58

the dead back to life. He told her to keep it clean. "Don't throw garbage at the foot of the tree, or it will fly away," he warned her many times.

At first his wife did as she was told. But by and by she got angry with her husband for showing more love for the tree than for herself. She was tired of his warnings too. So one day, when they had a quarrel about the tree, she lost her temper and shouted: "I'll throw garbage at the foot of the tree if I want to."

Angrily, she brought a bucket full of garbage from the kitchen and dumped it at the foot of the tree with a thud. Suddenly the banyan tree began to shake. Gradually it pulled its roots out of the ground and began to rise in the air.

Seeing what was happening, Big Liar rushed to the tree and caught hold of one of the roots. But the tree kept rising. Up and up it soared, high into the sky, with Big Liar clinging to the root. And it went on flying until finally it reached the moon, where it has remained ever since.

If you look carefully at the moon, you can still see the shadow of the tree there, with Big Liar seated at its foot, especially when the sky is clear and the moon is full and bright. So say the people of Viet-Nam.

Retold by Nguyen Văn Y
Translated by Vu Trong Ung
Illustrated by Nguyen Thi Hop